We like to swing.

We like to whizz and spin.

We like to yell in tunnels.

We like to splish, splash and splosh.

We like to run in the sun and dig in the sand.

We like to squelch in the mud and stamp on the twigs.

9

We like to jump off a log and hit a stump with a stick.

We like to hop like frogs

and spring like squirrels.

And when we get home...

we like to flop.